THE
MAGICAL
STARFRUIT
TREE

A Chinese Folktale

Adapted by

ROSALIND C. WANG

Paintings by

SHAO WEI LIU

Beyond Words Publishing, Inc.

Published by
Beyond Words Publishing, Inc.
13950 NW Pumpkin Ridge Road
Hillsboro, Oregon 97124
Phone: (503) 647-5109
Toll-free: 1-800-284-9673

Art Direction and Design: Su Lund Studio

Printed in the United States
Distributed by Publishers Group West

Library of Congress Cataloging-in-Publication Data

Wang, Rosalind C.
    The magical starfruit tree / story by Rosalind Wang:
illustrations by Shao Wei Liu. p. cm.
    Summary: A stingy peddler is chastised for his
miserly ways by an old beggar with magical powers.
    ISBN 0-941831-89-2 : $14.95
    (1. Folklore—China.) I. Liu, Shao Wei, ill.
II. Title.
PZ8.1.W186Mag 1993
398.2'0951—dc20
(E)   93-3656   CIP   AC

The costumes, hairstyles, and settings depicted in
this book are representative of the Sung and Yuan
dynasties who ruled in China from 960-1368 A.D.
This was a very prosperous era in Chinese history.

*To my beloved parents, Chun-Hei Chou
and Shun-Yean H. Chou, and
their lovely grandchildren*

—R. C. W.

In memory of James Sanford

—S. W. L.

*The Magical Starfruit Tree is one of many traditional Chinese
folktales my parents told me as a young girl. These tales
entertained the children while introducing them to Chinese
culture and reinforcing moral values. This story still provides
me with inspiration and encouragement.*

—R. C. W.

Long, long ago in the southern part of China, there lived a fruit peddler named Ah-Di. He was so mean and so greedy that no one liked him. Yet his starfruit always grew so ripe and juicy that people from faraway lands would come to buy them in the market.

One summer day, the fruit peddler packed his two big baskets full of luscious yellow starfruit and rushed to the market. A great crowd had gathered because it was the monthly market day. They came to shop and to watch the acrobats perform. Ah-Di set up his fruit stand near the performers, under a yum-yum tree, and was pleased with himself for finding such a good spot. He murmured, "The day is very hot and dry. People will be thirsty. I shall sell every one of my ripe and juicy starfruit and make lots of money!"

Some people could not afford to buy his starfruit and could only look longingly at them. Ah-Di was so mean and nasty. He would yell at the poor bystanders, "Are you going to buy? If not, stay away! Don't block my fortune!"

Toward afternoon, an old man came along and stopped in front of the fruit stand. His faded green clothes were shabby, and he didn't have a penny in his pocket. All he had in his hand was a tree branch that served as his cane. He wore a straw hat atop his head, and his wrinkled face was covered with sweat and dust. But if you looked closely, you could see there was something different about this old man. When the sun shone into his dark brown eyes, they sparkled with a mysterious jade-green color.

The old man observed Ah-Di's juicy starfruit and said, "Oh good Fruit Peddler, I am very thirsty, but I have no money to buy your fruit. I believe that you are a kind-hearted man. Surely you will have mercy on an old man and give me a juicy starfruit."

"Go away, old beggar!" the stingy Ah-Di shouted. "My starfruit are for *sale*. They bring me wealth. I do not give my fruit away to anyone!"

"Oh good Fruit Peddler, have mercy on these old bones. I do not want your biggest and plumpest starfruit. All I want is the smallest one, one that you might throw away. I know the Jade Emperor of Heaven will bless you for your kindness."

"Who do you think you are?" Ah-Di yelled. "Why do I need *you* to ask the Jade Emperor to give me blessings? Go away before I beat you with my stick!"

People in the marketplace heard the noise and formed a circle around them.

"Shame on you, Fruit Peddler," said a bystander. "This old man is tired and thirsty. Give him a starfruit. It will not hurt you a bit, but a small fruit will quench his thirst. The Jade Emperor of Heaven will surely reward you for your kindness."

"That's right!" cried the crowd, "Have pity on the old man."

"Oh yes, saying is easier than doing!" yelled Ah-Di. "It is not *your* starfruit you give away so easily. You do not toil and labor to produce them! If you have such a kind heart, why don't you buy one and give it to this old beggar?"

At that moment, a young boy named Ming-Ming, one of the acrobats, had just finished his performance. He came forward with two copper coins and handed them to the stingy Ah-Di.

"I will buy a starfruit for the Lau Gong Gong (old grandpa)," said Ming-Ming. He then turned to the old man and said very kindly, "Lau Gong Gong, you may now select a large, juicy starfruit for yourself. Do not worry, I have paid the fruit peddler."

The old man hesitated, "How can I take your money? You have worked hard for these two coins."

"Lau Gong Gong, I do not have much, but I am willing to share what I have. I'll perform again, and most of these kind aunties and uncles will give me more money."

The old man selected a starfruit and ate it down to the core. He then carefully picked out one of the seeds and threw the rest of the core away.

"Ahhh, it is so good," he said as he smiled. "Thank you, little boy. You have been very kind to me. Now, please help me perform for our audience here."

The old man used his cane to dig a hole in the ground. In it, he placed the carefully selected seed and asked the boy to pack the earth over the seed with his two little feet.

"Now I need to water the seed. Can anyone here supply me with a pot of hot water?"

The crowd was puzzled by his request. It was such a hot day. The old man would kill the seed for sure!

"Are you sure you need *hot* water?" someone from the crowd exclaimed. People looked at each other, hoping someone would explain this peculiar logic. Some stood there quietly, while others shook their heads, thinking that the old man was simply light-headed from the heat. Finally, someone from the crowd handed over a pot of boiling water, which the old man sprinkled on the ground.

A tiny green shoot sprang up immediately.
As the crowd watched in awe, the plant grew taller
and taller and taller. Their eyes followed the plant
as it grew, and their heads tilted back farther and
farther and farther until they could no longer see
the top. They did not know exactly when the plant
stopped growing, but their necks were sore from
looking up.

The old man pointed his cane at the tree and said, "Leaves, my good tree, grow leaves!" and the tree instantly became an umbrella of green leaves, shading the crowd from the scorching sun.

While the crowd stood there dumbfounded, the old man pointed his cane at the branches of the tree and said, "Bloom, my good tree, bloom!" and the tree burst forth pink and violet flowers.

The crowd gasped in amazement. No sooner had they uttered oohs and ahhhs of wonder, when once again, the old man pointed his cane at the tree and said, "Fruit, my good tree, bear sweet and juicy fruit!" A gentle breeze swept over the tree and blew the beautiful blossoms down upon the crowd. In place of the flowers, big, bright starfruit appeared on the branches.

By then, the news of this strange happening had spread quickly throughout the marketplace. Everyone, including Ah-Di, rushed over and gathered around the old man and his amazing tree.

After calming the restless crowd, the old man turned to Ming-Ming and said, "It is your turn to perform. Please use your nimble feet to climb up into the branches and gather the juicy starfruit for all of us."

Obediently, the boy climbed up the tree trunk like a little monkey. He picked the starfruit and passed them out to all the bystanders. Even the stingy peddler received his share. Ah-Di thought to himself, "Hmm...that's funny! This starfruit is as sweet and juicy as those in my baskets."

After everyone enjoyed their starfruit, the old man picked up his cane and struck the tree trunk several times. Each blow made the tree shrink smaller and smaller until it was the size of his palm. He then gave it to Ming-Ming and said, "Thank you for your assistance, little fellow. Plant this tree in your yard and you will have plenty of starfruit to quench your thirst every summer." Ming-Ming thanked him, and the old man picked up his cane, bowed to the audience, and walked through the crowd and down the dusty road.

Stunned by the series of strange happenings, people rubbed their eyes. They could hardly believe what they had seen. They even licked their lips to assure themselves that they had indeed eaten one of the sweet, juicy starfruit.

Suddenly, Ah-Di remembered his unattended fruit baskets. With all these people, he could still sell more fruit. But when he looked into the baskets, they were empty. His high-pitched scream filled the air.

"My starfruit! My starfruit!" cried the mean, stingy Ah-Di. "All my starfruit are gone from my baskets! It must have been that wretched old man who took my fruit and gave them to the crowd. Oh! Oh! All my wealth is gone!"

Leaving his two empty baskets behind, Ah-Di ran down the dirt road as quickly as he could to look for the old man. But alas! The only thing he found was the tree branch that the old man used as a cane, lying alongside the road.

The crowd broke into laughter at the greedy Ah-Di.

"That old man must have been a messenger sent down by the Jade Emperor of Heaven to teach that mean fruit peddler a lesson," said one person.

"That stingy fruit peddler deserves this for the way he treated the old man," said another person.

Yes, yes, the crowd all nodded in agreement. The Jade Emperor of Heaven is wise and just. Those who do not have a kind heart and respect for the old will surely be punished. But those who care about others and share what they have will surely be rewarded.

"NATIVE PEOPLE, NATIVE WAYS" Series
Author: Gabriel Horn, Illustrator: Shonto Begay

Wisdom and information from the Native American oral tradition are passed to the children of this generation through this series of stories about the history, heroes, culture, and traditions of the American Indians. The series is designed around the Native American symbol of the Circle of Life. Each of the Four Directions in the circle symbolizes a certain power: East is knowledge, South is life, West is the power of change, and North is wisdom.

Native American Book of KNOWLEDGE—Investigates the fascinating origins of the Native American people and introduces readers to key figures in the history of the Americas, including Deganawida, Hyonwatha, and many other Native American heroes.

Native American Book of LIFE—Teaches about Native American children: their pastimes, how they're named, initiated, taught, disciplined, and cared for; and about food in the culture: how it is grown and gathered, feasting traditions, and food contributions.

Native American Book of CHANGE—An important historical look at the conquests of the Toltec, Aztec, Mayan, and North American tribes; and a lesson about commonly believed stereotypes of Native Americans and others.

Native American Book of WISDOM—Explores the fascinating belief system of Native Americans—from the Great Mystery to the belief that all life is sacred and interrelated—and the magical traditions and power of this people.

Fifth- to sixth-grade reading level. 96 pages, $4.95 per volume, softcover

COYOTE STORIES FOR CHILDREN: Tales from Native America
Author: Susan Strauss, Illustrator: Gary Lund

Native American coyote tales interspersed with true-life anecdotes about coyotes and Native wisdom. This cycle or small "saga" of coyote's adventures during "the time before the coming of the human beings" illustrates the creative and foolish nature of this popular trickster and demonstrates the wisdom in Native American humor. Whimsical illustrations weave between the text.
Ages 4-12, 48 pages, $6.95 softcover, $10.95 hardbound

THE LAND AND THE PEOPLE: Republic of China
Photographer: Tim Harmon, Introduction: Madame Chiang Kai-shek

The photographer was granted permission to journey to areas of Taiwan formerly restricted to foreigners. His sensitive images capture the feelings of the land, its people in both work and play and the spirit that inspires this country. Included are ground-breaking photos which glimpse into the lives of seven aboriginal tribes living as they have for the past ten thousand years. Accompanied by an entertaining and informative text.
144 pages, 114 color and 5 black and white photos, $39.95 hardbound